CAVEMAN DAYS
(Accidental Step into Time Machine)

Trista Kerne

TABLE OF CONTENTS

CHAPTER ONE

If I step through this glowing doorway the consequences could be catastrophic! The oscillating strobes were hypnotic as my feet carried me onto the entrance.

What if this was a *true time machine?* Should I risk everything on a whim just out of natural curiosity from words overheard? Cory had told my brother Rocco about his experiment. Apparently, it had worked! Rocco had convinced me that his friend had indeed built a real time machine. "Listen Jenna," he had said to me "this is not a joke! You are my sister, not a baby anymore however, I felt it was better to warn about going there; it is dangerous. Don't even think about it!"

His words echoed in my brain while I stood there. Before I had time to think deeply while teetering at the doorstep to the contraption, *momentum carried me forward.*

Oh no!

A moment of hesitation was lost as my *balance shifted too far inside*, initiating the terrifying tumble into the void!

Loud buzzing in my ears along with rough vibrations overwhelmed my senses. Just before consciousness winked out, an adrenaline shot created a **heat flash** of panic as a kaleidoscope of colors surrounded the world around me.

Mercifully, all became quiet.

As if awakening from a deep sleep, my brain struggled while gaining traction to absorb the input from all my senses. My eyes fought to focus on the new scenery which was so incredibly different. For a long time, I just lay on the ground trying to figure out what happened. I felt drool come out of my mouth. Drool or blood? The frightening realization that I had entered a time machine and emerged into a totally different environment shocked me into action.

This was real. Even the warm air smelled different with the high humidity.

Dear God! **What have I done?**

Where am I? Or more appropriately, *when* am I? When Rocco had told me about the time machine, I didn't really believe it, until now!

My life flashed before my eyes. Tears welled up as the emotion of regret overwhelmed me. Why did I go through the portal without being sure of the consequences? Slowly I sat up. After wiping my mouth, it was a relief to see that there wasn't any blood. A wave of dizziness began until I stifled it.

Could this be the end of my life already? As a beautiful twenty-six-year-old woman, it seemed such a waste of a good life. I wanted to undo what I had just done. Wasn't there a reset button somewhere? Having been brought up in a generation of instant gratification and games, the cold harsh reality that this was **real** set over me like a horrifying shockwave.

Where was the exit? There has got to be a way to return! Oh please God help me! Frantically I circled around searching for some type of door. With a racing pulse my mind was in a panic.

A loud screech from an enormous creature tore my self-pitying mind out of my trance. *What the hell was that?* A dinosaur bird? Holy shocker, how *far* back did I go back in time?

Oh no, the monster had *spotted* me! It began to circle around. Was I lunch? Not one to helplessly allow myself to be eaten, I leaped up and then rushed for protection in the forest.

Thankfully, the cover of unfamiliar trees kept me out of sight from the gigantic bird. As I ran through along the strange terrain it suddenly occurred to me that I had been holding my cellphone in my right hand the whole time! How funny is that. As soon as I became aware of such a familiar item, I sat down to look at it. Still panting from the rush to apparent safety, I looked at the screen. Maybe by some miracle it would show me something.

Seriously I already knew that of course cellphone service would not exist in the past. And it would need gps satellites for location. Hesitantly I turned it on. As it powered up, I prayed out loud. My hands were still skaking.

The main display came on and just like I suspected, **no** service. Without Internet it was quite useless. *But wait*, **not** completely. At least the torch app could give light at night. And yes, my music library would still be there. I could take pictures, video or record sounds. The calculator might come in handy later. With a sinking feeling it also occurred to me that without a way for recharging nothing would work after the battery ran out! It was still at 99%, so I turned it off to save it only for when I would really need it.

The sounds all around me were scary and unfamiliar. What should I do? I needed a place to rest safely. How could I have been so dumb as to slip into a time machine? And to go backwards in time so hopelessly far. Why couldn't it have been the future? Maybe people there would have been nice to me.

Darkness was coming!

I was so very terrified. My legs were trembling. The only comfort was my cellphone just in case I needed light. The temperature was dropping quickly.

Strangely it became quieter. I wasn't sure if that was a good thing or a warning of danger. Through the openings in the trees, I saw the stars begin to show up. So bright!

Oh dear God, they were totally unfamiliar! **None** of the constellations looked right. The solar system was on another side of our milky way galaxy! The horrifying realization that I really was so far back in time caused a sinking feeling that I would quite possibly die alone here without a hope. Tears welled up and I began sobbing quietly. This was serious. Why had I so carelessly gone through the doorway? Life isn't some type of computer game. A powerful sense of hopelessness and fear came over me. I closed my eyes to try blocking out the terrifying situation.

Exhaustion overtook my body as I eventually fell asleep on the ground.

CHAPTER TWO

Next morning, I awoke to brilliant morning sunshine. The sobering reality of my predicament presented many options. Should I feel sorry for myself and wither and then die slowly, or should I make the best of it. *I decided to survive.* While reaching to scratch my head something made me jump. Oh, just my sunglasses! Apparently, I had them on my head the whole time yesterday without feeling them. Well, that was a tiny bit of positive news. At least I could protect my eyes from the sun.

What a waste. Here I was all alone. Such a pretty girl without anyone to talk to. I missed social media, and the news. I missed people. Guys and girls.

I looked down at myself. Yes, I was beautiful in my slim jeans and lovely t-shirt. I had worn socks with sneakers. No bra because my breasts were quite small. I like them like that. Although some people made a big deal about big breasts, I didn't worry about that and even noticed that a lot of people didn't even seem to notice. The sporty look suited my long blonde hair. I loved my body. But what use was my beauty without anyone to appreciate it?

Just as I got up to find a place to pee, an object fell from the tree above me. What was that? I felt something sticky in my hair and then grabbed it in fear. Please don't be animal feces! Just as I instinctively tossed it, I noticed it was a fig! I went to retrieve it and then opened it up. Yes, it was a ripe fig. Purple on the outside and beautiful on the inside. It smelled amazing. Wow, something to eat! I wouldn't starve. I tasted a bit of it. It was heavenly. This tree would be my home base. I had survived the night on the ground without being eaten, and this lovely tree would provide at least the basics to survive.

On the way to pee, I looked more closely at the types of trees nearby. One seemed to be an olive tree, and another seemed to have an orange fruit. Something to explore later.

I pulled down my jeans and panties to squat while doing my duties. There was no need for modesty. Perhaps I was the only human on earth. Anyway, I never had hang-ups about nudity. I drove my family crazy because I saw nothing wrong with the human body and didn't make huge efforts to cover up every time someone was around. Thinking of my family, I suddenly missed my parents and only sibling, my older brother, Rocco who was thirty.

A shelter of some sort would be needed. Even a fire would be necessary to cook anything and maybe for protection, especially after my cell phone battery died.

My brain was going through plans to make things more comfortable. First, I needed to construct a place to sleep. The ground was not my thing.

I guess I had all the time in the world. No clock, no deadlines. Well actually the deadline was the *darkness.*

No money, no identification, and only the clothes I was wearing. How long could I make them last? A few months if they didn't get too tattered. I decided to find water. It occurred to me that perhaps that would be my main goal for today. I became thirsty.

As I walked along, I made sure to leave a trail of twigs so that I could find my fig tree without getting lost. For what seemed like an hour, I explored. In the distance I heard a sound of running water. It was exciting to hear it. I ran along while focusing on the whooshing flow. Just as I was about to approach it, a figure *jumped* about twenty feet in front of me.

I screamed and slid to full stop. With heart racing I froze in place. What the ...?

It was a **cave man!** Are you kidding me? I was terrified. So was he. I saw the fear in his eyes. We both stood in place staring at each other. As his gentle manner calmed me down, I considered my options. Should I run? I decided against that as I realized that he was bigger and stronger than me as well as more familiar with the terrain and could easily catch me if a pursuit ensued.

He was naked! And very hairy. His rugged features betrayed a rough existence. His penis was showing.

I decided to attempt communicating with him. Maintaining a safe distance, I smiled first and then said, "Hello?"

What did I expect? It would be too funny to expect a caveman to understand English. Silly me.

He simply grunted back with a puzzled expression. And then he turned around and took off!

"Wait," I pleaded. Too late, he was gone. It was funny that he was more scared of me than I was of him. In fact, I was so relieved to make contact with another human being. I was happy. Thank god I wasn't alone in the world. Maybe there were many like him around. Surely, they wouldn't just kill me. I wasn't an animal and although I must have looked like an alien from outer space to him, at least I was pretty. I was certain he knew I was a female although my tiny breasts didn't show well.

For a long time, I just sat there. After a while I decided to approach the babbling brook to drink pure fresh water. It was cool and refreshing as I used my cupped hands to scoop it up and felt like an animal as the water dripped down my chin.

While I was here at the amazing stream, I decided to clean up. I removed all clothing and did my best to rinse off the stains. I shouldn't get them wet completely because I didn't have a change of clothes and couldn't imagine walking around in soaking wet jeans. I splashed water on my face and underarms. Without soap it was quite a rudimentary cleaning but better than allowing smells and bacteria to grow on me.

On the way back I was momentarily confused at one point because I had forgotten which way to turn to get back to my fig tree. Because the sun's position had changed, I made a mistake and had to backtrack all the way to the creek. Eventually I saw the trail of twigs!

At the fig tree I decided to climb it for safety. Just for tonight because there wasn't enough time to build anything. I ate my fill of figs and olives as well. A strange diet perhaps leading to diarrhea, but better than starvation.

CHAPTER THREE

After sleeping uncomfortably in the tree all night, I felt sore and miserable and then jumped down to pee.

There had to be a way to store water. Would I forever have to go all the way to the creek for quenching my thirst? Too far. There had to be a better idea.

A rustling in the bush caught my attention. Alarm bells in my head warned me to climb the tree really fast. Just as I was frantically grabbing branches, I saw it. A horrifying creature with pointy scales like a wild sort of boar. It hadn't noticed me. I could see that it was just scurrying around probably looking for food. An idea formed in my head about using a spear to hunt something like that. My survival instinct had changed me from a girly girl into a hunter!

After it had left, I jumped out of the tree to make my trek to the water.

CHAPTER FOUR

The creek was truly a beautiful place. I removed my clothes and then carefully stepped in for a swim. With water at a comfortable temperature, it was a thrill to swim around until my mind imagined that it was too good to be true and perhaps something might grab me for dinner. Maybe a snake! My imagination ruined the paradise as I leaped out panting in fear while looking carefully back at the water. Nothing there. I would need to relax.

Again, I washed my clothes a bit. What would I do about soap? The urge to look it up on the Internet as a force of habit came up until I realized, no Internet. I should have appreciated the world before where information was available at my fingertips for free anytime. What a spoiled brat I had become. As they say, you don't miss anything until it is gone.

Just before getting dressed I noticed my reflection in the water. Wow, was that gorgeous girl really me? For a long time, I looked at myself. So sad if my life would become just a battle to survive. Surely this wasn't my future.

I wondered if there might be a way to go back to my time in the future. After all the time machine had dropped me here, maybe the door to go back was still there. Where had I landed the first time? Perhaps I could retrace my steps and remember where exactly I found myself. Maybe I should return there and look around. Suddenly I was hopeful.

After putting on my clothes, I tried to figure out where that monster bird had chased me into the forest. I remembered that it was a clear area leading up to my fig tree. As I recalled my trajectory while running from the bird had been mostly in a straight line.

After searching for what seemed like hours, I saw the place. I knew it was the one because a hairpin had fallen out of my blonde locks. I picked it up and examined it. Yes, it was mine! I shook off the dirt and pinned it back into my hair. Yes, this was the spot. My shoe prints showed in some soft ground on the way to the forest.

So, this was exactly where I had landed from the future. While turning around and frantically scanning every detail, I realized there was nothing unusual. I walked around in ever expanding circles just in case I stumbled onto something. I looked up and around in every direction. I pressed the ground for soft spots.

Nothing. No sign of anything out of place. Since it was getting I late I decided to head back to my figs!

I climbed up and then contemplated my situation. Curiosity about the caveman had me hopeful that maybe I should try to find someone like him to seek companionship with. I had become so lonely that I caught myself talking out loud.

My life had been so easy before. It had been effortless to make friends. I was an open-minded woman and had enjoyed relationships with males and females. Boyfriends came naturally to me. Having gained a lot of experience over the years had led to a rich inventory of knowledge about how to deal with people. Of course, a lot of it was due to my physical beauty however I didn't feel guilty about that because life is not meant to be fair.

Thinking back on my awesome sexual experiences had me aroused in the tree. Many boyfriends had given me extreme pleasure, especially the older ones. And I had also learned how to give incredible satisfaction to guys as well. It had been fun. For some reason I thought of that fearful but ruggedly attractive cave man. Would I ever see him again? Surely his curiosity would get the best of him.

CHAPTER FIVE

Storm clouds on the horizon convinced me to make an attempt at building a crude shelter. I considered looking for a cave but changed my mind when I imagined what might be hiding inside. Perhaps I shouldn't have watched so many horror movies.

An odd thing about this place was a lack of insects. I could see any bugs! So weird. No songbirds, just the odd screech every now and again.

Without an axe or even a knife, it was looking mighty difficult to cut branches for making a shelter. Thinking back to my history lessons it occurred to me that a sharp rock could be used for cutting things.

A trip back to the water allowed me to quench my thirst and then look around the shoreline for rocks. I settled on two pointy lightweight pieces of shale and then stuffed them into my back pockets after moving my cellphone into my front pocket.

Upon returning to my fig tree, I set about cutting branches of a smaller bush to make a rudimentary bed against the larger tree trunk nearby. It was difficult but worked. Then it was time to form a lean-to structure to protect from the elements. As I paused to look around, I noticed a grape vine! I was excited not only for the fruit but the rope qualities of the tough looking vine.

It worked well! I was so proud of myself for getting into the caveman construction business. The branches and vines formed a dreadful yet comfortable looking shelter. I stood back and admired my new home and even turned on my phone for a minute to take a selfie with it.

With my self-confidence soaring I decided to try making a fire. First, I gathered dry pieces of vegetation. Then used the pointy rock to form a tiny rod. Remembering my girl guide days, I began twirling the wood back and forth. It took forever to see a tiny wisp of smoke. Soon I became too tired to continue. It would have to wait until later.

Time to try something easier. I formed a strange looking hook out of a twig and then attached it to a vine. With a fig on the hook for bait it was time to try fishing!

I walked all the way to the stream and then cast out. It looked quite ridiculous, yet at least I was trying something.

Unbelievably I got a hard bite within a few minutes. Not wasting my chance, I pulled hard to set the hook while backing up to pull it ashore. Oh, dear lord it was an ugly large fish. It was scary to look at. Totally unfamiliar. There was no way I was going to touch it! I simply dragged it the distance to my shelter. It had died by that time. For a long time, I studied the large monster fish pondering whether it would be worth taking the chance to taste it. Well I would need to make a fire. I wasn't into the raw thing, no way.

I decided to use superhuman efforts to get a fire started. Eventually I got to see smoke again! This time I refused to give up. Fighting through the pain in my wrists, I saw the first tiny flame. YES! I kept it up until it caught. While frantically blowing on it I used my free hand to feed it slowly until a real fire had caught. It was a glorious moment of joy. I was so happy. The stockpile of larger and larger dry pieces of twigs and dead branches helped to make it grow.

The only way I could think of to cook the fish was to poke a stick through from the anus to the mouth and slowly roast while turning it slowly over the flames. In time the smell was quite pleasant and my hunger for protein had become overwhelming.

I used the rock to break it open to see if it was cooked. The steam from the inside showed that it was ready. With the ground as my plate I dared to reach inside. **Ouch**, too hot! Needs time to cool a bit.

Using leaves this time, I reached inside for a fillet. Carefully sniffing first, I then took a tentative bite. *It was delicious*. So very tasty even without salt or any flavorings. I was so hungry but took my time taking it apart piece by piece while separating the guts and bones. My girlie appearance must have changed by now with the juices dripping down my chin. It was difficult to stay clean without napkins or paper towels. There would be time to clean up at the water tomorrow.

CHAPTER SIX

Another day. Adapting to the outdoor living wasn't easy. I missed my easy life from before. How could I have taken it all for granted? "Oh lord, if ever I should get a chance to miraculously return, I swear my attitude would undergo a major shift."

While standing up I made another discovery in my pocket. A comb! Wow, it felt like such a luxury item as I turned it around to stare in disbelief. At last I could straighten out the tangles.

What else had I missed? Looking through all of my pockets I discovered some coins in the change pocket. Quite useless but perhaps intriguing for a caveman.

A sadness came over me as I thought of my parents and brother. I would never see them again. It was like they died. Perhaps I should have a ceremony of some sort. There had to be a way to have closure. The grief coursing through my mind was strong.

With the sharp rock, I dug a hole nearby and planted a cross. Then another two. Three altogether representing my parents and brother. After doing that I said a sweet prayer for then while sending my love forever. The tears welled up and rolled down my cheeks.

After contemplating my life, I sat there a long time.

A smell caught my attention. What was that? Oh darn, my feet were smelly. I guess walking in my damp socks inside wet shoes caused a stinky reaction, so I leaped up and then ran for the creek.

This time I made a special effort to rinse off my socks and shoes in the water and then left them to dry in the sun before putting back on. I looked at my bare feet and noticed that all toenails were too long. What would I do without nail cutters? I guess I would need to use my teeth. Yuk! But at least my body was still flexible to bend enough to bring my toes up to my mouth. Same with my fingernails, I would have to bite them.

It was bright this morning, so I put on my sunglasses. My skin needed lotion. I didn't want my face to age early! I remembered the caveman's face looking weathered. He was probably my age yet looked twice that.

While looking around I spotted a piece of wood almost like a large cup. With a little work from my stone at the fig tree maybe I could form a drinking cup so that I could finally store water instead of walking so far, every time I needed a drink.

After my shoes and socks had dried in the hot sun, I put them back on and then returned home. I left the wood for making a water container by my shelter to work on tonight as darkness would settle in. For now, I thought of a great plan. I would make a spear for hunting small animals.

It was easy to find a straight and strong branch to sharpen and shape. After working on it, the weapon looked great. This could even be used for self-defense. I could make a stockpile for later use. For now, I decided to go hunting. The balance was good as I practiced throwing. It was fun! I learned how far I could safely aim for accuracy. About twenty feet or so.

Finally, it was time to hunt. I must have been quite an interesting sight sneaking through the forest with a spear in my right hand. I went in a straight line to avoid getting lost.

Where were all the animals hiding? I had seen that wild boar the other day but nothing else since. I heard the odd screech now and then. Were there any big dinosaurs around? Tyrannosaurus rex? Yikes! It was too quiet. Maybe they slept during the day and hunted at night. Perhaps I was just lucky not to be eaten by now. My imagination got carried away as I slowed down.

Suddenly I heard a rustling sound. I became fearful while crouching down to hide. Oh, I saw something big! What? The caveman! No, TWO cavemen together walking nearby. I saw them before they noticed me. Should I just let them pass by?

For some reason I wasn't afraid of them. They didn't appear to be armed.

"Hi there!" I blurted.

They both jumped out of their skin. The look of horror expressed by their facial expressions was priceless. Oh, please don't run away. I wanted to attempt communication. We made eye contact. I smiled. My sunglasses were still on. I must have been a frightening sight with those on.

While they were frozen in place, I slowly approached from about fifteen feet away. It had been so lonely for me, and I was painfully curious about them I couldn't let them run away. Surely since there were two of them a 'safety in numbers calculation' would have told them it was safe to stay a bit.

My wide smile must have told them to let me get closer. At about ten feet out I stopped and then reached into my back pocket to offer figs that I had wrapped in leaves for in case I got lost and needed food. They almost ran when I had reached back but held their ground. Carefully I bent down and extended the gift for them. They looked at each other while grunting in cave man talk.

Even though they were completely naked, I felt safe. It seemed they were unaware about their nudity. Society had not brainwashed them into thinking it was shameful. I liked their innocence. Just like I had been back home with my family, I was the same. This was a big plus for me. It would be a joy to befriend these masculine works of art. For sure they would have been wondering what type of creature I might be. My jeans and t-shirt would appear odd. Even my shoes would have been an unbelievable sight in their eyes.

They were barefoot and quite rugged looking. Both about the same height, perhaps related. Hairy bodies looked handsome and attractive. Their penises were quite small with tiny testicles. Long straggly hair and unkempt fingernails betrayed a primitive existence.

While carefully approaching my extended hand, they accepted and then retreated. I stayed low so that they would relax. Each sniffed and then took a bite and then finished eating the figs. They watched to see what I would do next.

My heartrate had increased substantially but this was exciting. How could I question them? No common ground.

While touching my chest, I said "Jenna."

They were puzzled. I moved closer and sat down cross-legged facing both.

Again, I patted myself. "Je," "Nah."

Then I pointed a finger to the one on the right. He seemed to get it! He said "Turuck!" I pointed to the other one. They looked at each other and then he said "Gabba!"

Just like a teacher I repeated "Jenna," while pointing to myself and them repeating to them, "Turuck," and then finally "Gabba."

They were pleased. I noticed they were staring at my body. My blonde hair shining in the sunlight. Oh yes, darn my sunglasses were still on. Slowly I moved them from covering my eyes to up on my head. They seemed to realize that I was indeed a human after all. They gazed into my eyes.

Suddenly a rustling sound revealed one of those boars approaching. We all stood up and then I grabbed my spear. As it appeared to be after Gabba, I aimed directly at it and then shot my spear. What a crazy shot. I got it right through its ear and it dropped dead right at Gabba's feet. Turuck and Gabba looked at me in wonder. I'm not sure they had ever done such a thing. I felt powerful and self-confident.

Since we weren't too far from my fig tree home, I decided to show off a little more. After removing the spear from the pig's head, I grabbed a hind leg and began dragging it to my place while beckoning the cave men to follow me.

It was heavy but I persevered. I didn't know how to ask for help and they didn't seem to understand what I was up to. Fortunately, they did follow me. As we arrived, I was happy to see that my fire was still smoking. I let go of the animal and then stirred up the flames. I threw on dry branches and a log. They seemed mesmerized by my skills. Had they figured out how to start a fire yet? Judging by their actions apparently not!

I used to sharp stone to cut open the animal and then arranged a meaty chunk onto a spit just like I had done with the fish. We would eat well today and at least I would have someone to share with! For the first time in a long time I was feeling good. They were patient while I turned it over and over. The smell was amazing. After it was done, I set it down to cool off while gathering leaves for plates.

It was time to enjoy a feast. I divided the sizzling meat into three and then served them. They weren't aware of manners as they chomped and grunted while the drippings went in all directions. I took a bite. It was delicious. Oh god so heavenly. The taste was even better than the great fish yesterday. After we were done, they looked at me with more curiosity. Probably I was the most interesting thing to happen to them during their entire lives. They looked happy and relaxed. After a while I didn't even notice that they were naked. Here I was, a beautiful girl sitting with two naked cavemen and yet it seemed innocent and natural.

Turuck looked up at the sky and pointed out an approaching storm. Gabba grunted. They looked at each other gesturing and making strange guttural sounds and then they simply took off! I was stunned. Well, I guess for a first date they sure made an impression on me as well. Looking up at the dark cloud blocking the sun, I realized I was in trouble. I dragged the carcass over the fire to finish cooking the rest because I knew the fire might be washed out soon. Darn, the storm ruined my chance for socializing. I was sad.

I was so thirsty but couldn't take a chance on getting caught in a thunderstorm. It would have to wait until tomorrow. While waiting for the storm I thought about the cavemen. They now knew for sure where I was staying and would likely return. At least I hoped so. I missed them already.

A bright flash of lightning told me to run into my tiny shelter. A deafening boom of thunder followed. No rain yet. Remarkably the storm just missed my site. Thunder and lightning all around yet not over me! Amazing. My fire stayed. The pig slowly roasted overnight.

I slept deeply while having many dreams. Missing my old life had a big influence on me as I dreamt about my brother and my apartment. I had been living alone before this time travel thing. My latest boyfriend had just broken up with me and I had been in a depressed mood. That was why I was so easily seduced by the forbidden time machine my brother had warned me about.

CHAPTER SEVEN

I woke up super early. My thirst was unbearable. In the semi-darkness I ran for the stream.

The early morning was magnificent. Silent with a fresh scent of flourishing vegetation. I cupped my hands and then drank like there was no tomorrow. It tasted cool and satisfying.

Here back in time there were no laws. No government, no taxes, but no doctors as well. I needed to be careful. No antibiotics or hospitals. Obviously if I got badly injured, I would suffer the fate of any creature in the wild if they became slow from old age or showing signs of difficulty. I remembered my grandfather had told me that in nature you won't often find an old animal, or even under the sea, same thing. Most creatures die from tooth and claw. Almost everything gets eaten and recycled!

I sat on the shoreline thinking about how to proceed with my life. The cavemen had presented an entertaining distraction for now. I wondered how we might connect again.

While sitting there lonely I pulled out my cellphone and then turned it on. After it powered up, I saw only 87% power left. Hey, what's that about, I barely used it. Anyway, I recorded a message to the future if any modern civilization ever found my phone after I die. I took a short video of my surroundings and then explained my situation. I expressed love for my parents and brother as well as my close friends and other relatives. The message ended with genuine tears.

A large spider crept by. It was scary but it seemed to be minding its own business. Snakes would scare me more. Just the thought of one slithering by gave me the creeps.

I drank more water and then walked back to my home base. I reached for olives to munch on while walking by the tree. They were really good.

At the fire I poked a stick to see how the pig was doing. Apparently, it was perfectly done and very tender. Cooking slowly all night was the trick.

A dramatic thought entered my head. Maybe I could invent something. Yes, how about the wheel! Why not? After all I had already impressed a couple of cavemen with my hunting and cooking skills. Even fire making had shocked them. My self-esteem was high. I reached into the pig with a stick and scooped out a well-done piece of meat. With my eyes closed I savored the taste.

In the forest my good hearing picked out something approaching. I picked up my spear while retreating towards my shelter. A fight or flight adrenaline response had me ready for anything.

It was Gabba and Turuck! They brought me a beautiful flower! Wow, even a caveman knew how to seduce a woman. Turuck handed it over to me. I accepted while smiling my sweetest ever smile. I bowed my head. "Thank you!" Of course, they wouldn't understand but I felt better saying the words.

I gestured towards the pig and encouraged them to help themselves. Gabba looked over and then sniffed the nicely done meat.

Without more prodding they began to eat while grunting and generally making a mess of it. I took more for myself and ate quietly.

Since there were no dishes to wash, I decided to liven up the party by turning on my cellphone and then locating the music app. As soon as the song came up, they both leaped up in fear! Gabba placed his hands over his ears. Laughing out loud I turned down the volume and then selected a softer tune. This time the reaction was more positive. Turuck cocked his ears sideways and focused on the phone. They couldn't believe what they were hearing.

I got up to dance! They watched me with eyes the size of dinner plates. I gyrated about in a provocative manner while turning around and going up and down. It was such a fun time I almost forgot about the limited battery life. Oh dear, it got down to 66%. I switched it off. Sorry guys, party is over. As I looked at them, I realized again that I had forgotten that they were in the nude. I was totally into judging them by character only without a thought for their physical appearance. They smelled bad up close, but I couldn't blame them for ignorance about personal hygiene.

There was a lot to learn about these guys. I needed to find out where they lived and if there were more of them. Surely it wasn't just the two of them. I briefly wondered if they were gay because neither one had made a move on me. Maybe they weren't sure if I was a human female. If they thought I was a friendly sexless alien that would explain a lack of interest in me as a woman.

To test my hypothesis, I reached out to touch Gabba's hand. At first, he recoiled but then returned his hand to mine. I ran my fingers across his open palm. Immediately I spotted a sexual response as his penis jumped and began to swell. Oops, I'd better be careful. These guys might get the wrong idea. I put on the brakes by retrieving my hand and gesturing that it was time for me to sleep. I placed my hands together and rested my hand on them with closed eyes. Just for effect I made a fake snoring sound. They understood that it was time to go! Amazing. As they rose to leave, I waved bye. Turuck and Gabba waved back while making their way into the forest.

CHAPTER EIGHT

This morning I was in a better mood than yesterday at the same time. My new friends had given me hope for a better life ahead. As I tidied up my home, I noticed that juice had fermented into a hollow opening in the bark right behind where the shelter met the fig tree. I took a sniff and the distinctive smell of alcohol shocked me. Oh yes, I also missed getting drunk occasionally. Should I take a chance and drink it? Was it safe? Oh, what the heck. I pressed my lips against the opening and then sucked it in. It was very black and strong tasting but seemed oddly familiar. I ran my tongue over my lips to taste it better. Yes, it was definitely alcoholic.

In a few minutes, the signs of alcohol entering my bloodstream became unmistakable. Tingly lips and becoming a bit tipsy along with blurring vision showed the strong effects. I needed more! It was so enjoyable. Memories of crazy fun parties aroused my senses. Although alcohol was supposed to be a depressant, for me it was triggering a response of heightened arousal. Sexual arousal. I jumped around waving my hands like a bird. I was happy beyond belief without a worry in the world. For the first time since going back in time, I was feeling beautiful and free.

I heard a sound in the forest which momentarily had me concerned as I picked up a rock ready to wipe out any enemy.

It was Gabba and Turuck again! The rock slipped out of my hand and then fell to the ground. I was thrilled to the highest heights while giving each hug. They were shocked at my new attitude. Did they have any idea about alcohol? I gestured toward the tree and then reached down to suck the last drops of alcohol out of it. The puzzled expression on their faces was so funny. Suddenly I was super thirsty. We would have to go to the stream. Although so far away, I wanted them to join me. I grabbed their hands and ran with them all the way to the stream. Then cupped my hands to drink a ton of water. They did the same. I saw they were panting from the quick trek. A one hour walked condensed into twenty minutes.

I became super sexually aroused. What am I going to do? I needed release so badly. They watched my antics with a detached curiosity. I lost all inhibitions and began to remove my clothes. First my shoes and socks. Then my top. As soon as I pulled it over my head to toss it aside, all eyes were immediately on my tiny breasts! I loved the attention. Both of them grew erections! Those penises were not so tiny after all. Then I unsnapped my jeans while unzipping with my other hand. As I pulled them off, I gathered my panties at the same time and then stepped out of both my jeans and panties! **I was naked!** And so incredibly horny. Both cavemen sported raging erections as they realized that I was a real woman and not an alien. I wasn't sure how to proceed from here. I was drunk enough not to worry about pregnancy. Who cares at this point? It would be awesome to have a baby. Yet with two excited cavemen instead of one, I was a bit shy.

Gabba made the first move. He went behind me for a rear entry. I was willing to accept sex from him, but not from behind. I considered just giving them oral sex however my own needs required intercourse. Zero chance of oral for me, so no foreplay; however that was fine with me. Probably no chance of catching an STD, so never mind about unprotected sex. Just as he was about to enter, I turned around while pulling him on top of me as I lay down on my back. He couldn't understand so I took his hard rod and gently inserted it through my unshaven yet neat bush into my vagina.

The shock of a bare penis sliding into me sent extraordinary pleasure waves along the walls of my well lubricated vagina. I pulled him tight and helped him begin pumping. Finally, he understood as he began trembling while thrusting deep inside me. It was too much of a shock for him and he prematurely exploded wildly as he grunted and yelped. I could feel his intense climax as his bum clenched tightly. With wide eyes he held still while depositing a large volume of sperm into my unprotected pussy.

I was super aroused as well, yet it hadn't been enough stimulation for me to climax. I knew *then* that it was indeed fortunate that Turuck was here. I needed him to arouse me over the edge. Gabba rolled off in as if in a trance from the afterglow. I saw Turuck standing there totally freaked out at what just occurred. I reached up to him and he immediately jumped on top of me. No foreplay from this guy. The rough manner turned me on because I had been so close to climaxing before, and now sensed a chance for a natural orgasm for myself! He was so wild and different than Gabba. He shoved his rock-hard member inside and began pumping right away. His larger penis had stimulated every nerve ending inside the walls of my vagina sending waves of incredible pleasure through me. I arched my back towards him. My toes curled.

His steady rhythm indicated that he would last longer that Gabba had. Excellent. I was so drunk and hot. Perspiration dripped from his face. His musky smell was awesome. I raised my arms above my head in total surrender. The irreversible road to my own climax began in earnest.

A hot flash of extreme orgasmic pleasure signaled my approaching satisfaction. My lower body began trembling from the onslaught of a powerful climax. The feeling was unbelievable. I'd had sex with many different guys however something about this pulsating orgasm caused vibrations and leg trembling as I moaned loudly. I brought my arms down and used my hands to force him to pump deeply into me so that his own pleasure would increase. My soft feminine hands on his hairy bum sent him into a frenzy.

I sensed a quickening pace. Yes, he was about to explode inside of me. His breathing increased as his facial expression showed a serious focus while enjoying an awesome climax. I knew he was almost there as he stiffened up and held still while beginning to ejaculate big wads of semen into me. He grunted and shook hard as he shot load after load deep inside. I could feel the force of the sperm as it spurted strongly over and over until it began to leak out from the excess which ran all the way down along my perineum to my anus. I moaned again as a second orgasm shook me. My own pleasure from seeing him have his way with me had sent me over the top again. How could such an ecstatic pleasure be possible. As he rolled off me panting, we just all lay there in the afterglow. This had been a whole-body experience.

CHAPTER NINE

Remarkably I had fallen asleep naked on my back and had stayed that way all night until the sunlight woke me up the next morning. Turuck and Gabba had left.

Slowly I sat up and stretched. I felt okay considering the wild antics from the night before. Thank God the water was nearby to quench my thirst.

Oh wow, their sticky sperm had covered my pubic hair and was still coming out to run down my legs as I stood up. Out of a funny curiosity, I picked up some and sniffed. Yup, normal musky semen without a doubt. I was happy about the experience. At least it gave me hope that if I were going to spend the rest of my life here, at least a beautiful sex life would be possible. I was aroused just daydreaming about a repeat performance in the future. Please cavemen, come back and let's do it again!

The water looked cool today, but I needed to wash up before getting dressed. As I stepped into the creek, I noticed how clean the water was. I could see all the way to the bottom. Without soap I spent extra time just rubbing my body and splashing myself. I felt strong today, full of energy.

As I was getting dressed, I thought of how wonderful it would have been to have a coffee right now! I could just taste it. Perhaps there was a coffee bean bush somewhere. I would certainly begin exploring, perhaps starting with help from my cavemen friends. I wondered, were there any other females around? Would they be jealous or friendly? I missed female companionship. It would be great just to see a woman.

I became hungry and realized that food was so far away. I made a decision to relocate my shelter here by the creek. I would gather figs and olives and oranges and store them in my shirt by hold it up like a container. For the fire I would have to construct a pit with kindling and wood near the water. I spotted a large tree to prop my new shelter up. I would get more vines from the grapes to use as rope. There were plenty of different rocks here to be able to make more weapons. Maybe I could even make a crossbow. That would be cool.

On the way to my fig tree, I saw a strange glow come down from the sky. *What the heck was that?* I **froze** in my tracks. The radiance became a pulsating archway which settled about twenty feet ahead of me. It looked just like the time machine entrance from before! OMG! *Was this a way to return?* My quickening pulse shocked me into action. I ran towards it before it could disappear. Maybe my only chance to get back! Just as I was about to jump inside, I looked back and noticed the sky collapsing. Without any more hesitation, I leaped forward into the void and promptly lost consciousness.

In a daze I woke up. Sense of time was distorted. My body felt strange. My eyesight was clear as I focused on my new surroundings. I was inside the lab! Yes, I was back! Or was I? Slowly I stood up and looked around. Scratching my head, I examined the surroundings. It was odd. No noise at all. I reached into my back pocket for my phone. It was missing! It must have fallen out as I was running.

There was a door ahead. Just as I was about to open it, my brother came through!

"Rocco!" I ran to him and then jumped to encircle his entire body with my legs and hugged hard while tears streamed down my face. "Oh god I missed you so much! I love you. I thought I would never see you again! So sorry I ignored you warning about the time machine. It really worked. I can't believe I'm back!"

He seemed surprised by my reaction. I held on to him a long time. "I missed you too Jenna!"

Just then Cory entered the room. "Hi Jenna, nice to have you back!"

I let go of Rocco and went over to hug Cory as well. I had never been close to Cory however since I was a changed person, he received the same hug I did for Rocco. "Hi Cory, nice to see you!"

He was trembling with my deep hug. I guess I got carried away and had rubbed his bum while bringing my tear-filled face near his. I was so relieved to be back to safety that my emotions were in overdrive. He had wrapped his arms arm me tightly and it felt good.

I had so many questions about the time machine. How had they figured out how to bring me back? Cory offered me a coffee as we exited the room to enter Cory's lab. Yes, coffee! What a comforting thought.

Over the next few hours Cory and Rocco explained something unbelievable to me. They admitted that I had *never* actually gone back in time. With extreme guilt they told me about how they had drugged me to attach sophisticated virtual reality equipment to my body. My iris was fitted with an artificial intelligence lens which had generated the scenery all around me. The entire environment had been created ahead of time.

It was a shock to learn how I had been tricked so cleverly. I had been fooled completely. My anger grew by the minute, but I had to understand not only how they had done it but WHY?

Their vague answers only fueled my rising rage. They both tried to calm me down and assured me that there was no intention for harm. Only scientific curiosity about if the new VR would work opening up possibilities for a gigantic market to earn **billions.**

I calmed down a bit when I realized that they hadn't forced me to enter the machine, and I did emerge without any physical harm. A tiny capitalist section of my brain picked up on the word 'billions' and wondering about my part in all this.

I asked about the animals that I saw. They explained that everything was computer generated. Even when I had speared that pig, they made sure I didn't miss. When I made a fire, it was all a simulation. Smells and sounds were fake. But how about the food I ate. That was fake also. They had made sure I got my nutritional needs met from the fake figs and other things. Insects would use too much computational power, so they were omitted.

It was all making sense.

Except for one major thing. The cave men! What was that all about. OMG they had seen my reaction for everything. I blushed while realizing my sexual needs would been on display for all to see! The booze was real and the plan to get me drunk backfired, but they did take advantage of my vulnerable state. The plan had been to simply relax me. The sex was accidental. That was why they decided to bring me back prematurely.

They carefully explained that in order for me not to be depressed, cavemen had to enter the picture. But how did they seem so real? Cory said that they used stand-ins to make them more realistic. Who did they use? "Don't tell me you were the stand-ins!" I screeched. Are you kidding me? My brother was one of the cavemen?

"No no no, I swear it wasn't your brother. Incest is not his thing, so please remove that possibility from your mind."

"So who were the stand-ins?"

"Well this is hard to admit."

"Who!"

Cory looked embarrassed so I knew he was one. "Actually, I was one."

"Oh man, are you serious? I hate you!"

"Listen Jenna, I'm so sorry, no harm intended."

"Who was the other one? Tell me now or I'll freak!"

"You don't know him Jenna, it is not important."

I stormed out of the room totally flustered. As soon as I left out the door into the real world, I regretted being so harsh. But I was angry for being used like that. It was so nice to get outside into the fresh air. Not a simulation but the present. I was appreciative of everything around me as I made my way to my apartment.

After entering I sat down and thought about the crazy happenings of the last week. I reached for my phone. Darn it was left back in time, no wait a minute, there was no back in time. Where was my phone? I needed to call my parents. And catch up on the world. What about my girlfriend Vickie and all the rest? They must be worried about me. How long was I away?

As I was on my way back to Cory's lab to demand my phone back, Rocco had met me halfway. He already realized I depended on my phone and handed it to me. "Jenna, I love you please don't stay angry!"

I saw his dejected expression and melted. "Rocco I just need a little time to get over the shock of all this, I love you too so don't worry, I might forgive you." As I was saying that tears rolled down his cheeks.

Getting back to my cozy apartment I had a wonderful shower with real soap and then changed into clean clothes. I began to feel better about the whole situation. I made a coffee while chatting with mom and dad. I promised to be in touch with them more often in the future. I was a changed person. The experience had opened my eyes to what was important in life. My legacy was to be remembered as a good person who enjoyed life. The utter hopelessness of feeling trapped back in time had made me realize that there were many positives for living in our modern time. Heath care, security, and affordable creature comforts were to be appreciated more. Opportunities to have a successful life were there for the taking.

I had a super awakening and realized how life is precious.

CHAPTER TEN

After a good night's sleep, I found it in my heart to forgive Rocco and Cory. After getting myself all pretty and fresh, I walked over to see them. They were wary of my purpose. I could see the fear in their eyes. One by one I hugged them both and expressed a deep and genuine forgiveness.

Cory expressed regret at tricking me for so long. He also confessed that he had a secret crush on me since we met through my brother a few years ago.

It occurred to me that we had had sex together and although it was through a simulation, the feelings had been so real. He explained that the VR equipment was so realistic that intercourse would appear to be the real thing. Even the leaking semen had been created out of fancy graphics.

I couldn't believe that the pleasure had been so powerful. I remembered the vibrating orgasms I'd experienced. How could that be possible?

Apparently, the virtual reality effect had enhanced the sexual response because ninety percent of sex is in the mind! The real climax I felt was created mostly from the visuals and my active imagination.

"So, did we really have sex?"

"We didn't physically interact however the whole episode was played out using the most advanced artificial intelligence software imaginable. We were both attached to the simulation."

"Tell me Cory, um, did you also experience a climax?" I was curious.

"Honestly Jenna, I did experience the most mind-blowing orgasm of my life, and I'm thirty years old!"

"Cory, let me ask, which one were you, Gabba or Turuck?"

"I was Turuck."

"Oh, dear God, you were good! I still remember it clearly and I will treasure the memories forever!"

"Me too!"

"Just next time don't go to so much trouble to seduce me!" I laughed.

"Jenna, how about we go on a normal date?"

"Cory, let's try it!" I meant it, perhaps we would be compatible in true life as well, let's give it a go." Thinking of his wild antics back in time, I couldn't resist taking a chance with him.

Hand in hand we left for our first **real** date at the coffee shop!

THE END

OTHER BOOKS BY TRISTA KERNE

Wife with Strangers: Unexpected Cheating

Altered Thrills: Apocalyptic Bisexual Romance

Hidden Cam Surprise: Cheating Wife Caught

Artificial Transformation: A Transgender Fantasy Romance

Hotwife Cruise Vacation: A Shared Wife Adventure

First Time In Heat: Wife Surprise Cheating

Wife Overnight Camping: Accidental Cheating - First Time Taken

Sorry Honey: Accidental Wife Cheating

Accidental Cheating: Wife Infidelity

Cottage Party: Husband Sharing Erotic Romance Adventure

Island Strike: Husband Sharing His Wife

Class Reunion: Husband Caught Cuckquean Romance

Please consider leaving a review.

It would be delightful to receive an email from you! This is my private email account:

xhibitiongirl@gmail.com

I am open-minded and would love to receive comments (positive or negative) from my valuable readers! It is a pleasure to improve over time while adjusting to your feedback. Remember, I am just an individual, not a cold-blooded publisher just after your money! If you wish to remain anonymous it is okay, no problem. Perhaps you would like to join with me in writing a new title: YES! I am always open to that.

Thank you for reading this collection! It was fun writing these books. Although I am a 'finger-typer' and slightly dyslexic my wild imagination and dogmatic persistence guided my way. Take care...

All my *love* and **positive vibrations!**

Trista

Printed in Great Britain
by Amazon

26704946R00030